Kiss & Tell Tail 2

~o~

Reverse Harem Fairy Tales

Book 2

TIMEA TOKES

ISBN: 9798677788765

DEDICATION

To all my lovely readers out there. Remember, no matter what your dreams are (naughty or not), you have everything you need to make them come true.

If you love my writing style, please check out my other titles on Amazon, and follow me on my blog & website for a FREE pdf copy of Squirm Under My Watch, FREE Audiobooks, and other goodies, to say a personal thank you to you all.

I am also hosting a monthly signed paperback giveaway, with at least 2 winners each month. So, please stay tuned, and share the love that's deep inside all of you.

Thank you!

www.timeatokes.com

ACKNOWLEDGMENTS

All characters and events in these stories are purely fictional, therefore any resemblance to real people (living or dead) or events is a coincidence.

All characters would be at least 18 years of age, too, should they be real.

Caution: Contains descriptive sex scenes and adult contents.

Intended for a mature audience of at least 18+ (or more, depending on your country of residence and the local law).

Chapter 1

Someone please stop the noise. And get rid of the light. And the hammering in my skull. In fact, it might even be easier if that same someone just ended it all. Right here and right now. It doesn't sound like there is a much better fate waiting for me anyway. Lost memories, sea-witches and haunted dreams? And those desires I had...

My mind does a double take on me and the room begins to spin at full speed. In my mind's eye, I end up on the floor, holding on to it, thinking that I can't sink lower. A sinister thought tells me that I can and in fact, will sink even lower. I shake my head, reaching up, rubbing my forehead, but the pain intensifies, instead of going away. What's with me and the dreams? Don't even want to think about the headaches.

'You okay, love?'

Sebastian?

A shiver runs through me, and I think I'm still dreaming. The voice is smooth, and it makes me blush, especially because I remember the way he made me his just a moment ago (well, whether it actually happened and when it happened are both a mystery to me, but still). I try to sit up, but the now familiar pain shoots all the way down to my bum, then, resting there for a while, decides to travel all the way to my toes, tingling the little one. No, scrap that. This isn't tingling. This hurts like a motherfu...

Awesome.

'You scared us, you know. Are you sure you don't want me to call a doctor?'

No, he isn't Sebastian, and yet, I know him somehow. His voice is as familiar and as calming as the merman's, but instead of the ocean, it's velvety, flowing freely like a river. But how is this possible? As my eyes begin to demist, my mind clears along with my vision. Oh, it's Eric. The guy I'm supposed to kiss for some stupid reason.

Right.

'Um, I'm ok-kay.'

I slur a bit, but it doesn't matter. I'm getting up, even if the floor and the spinning room don't agree with me. Even if my own body doesn't agree with me and my mind cuddles the floor like an old friend. I'm horizontal when I'm with this guy way more often than I would like to be. It might be the dreams, I'm not sure, but for some reason, I have a really bad feeling about him. I just don't trust him.

And yet I would have sex with an imaginary creature. Awesome.

Call me crazy, but Eric seems even less real than the dreams and my merman. He might be handsome and caring and rich and whatever girls normally go for, but I guess I'm not your typical swoony woman who can be swept off her feet too easily. Well, by a guy I mean. Okay, fine, I might be on the floor, but that's not what I mean anyway.

And those dreams... Is the reason for my mistrust a previous lover I'm unable to let go of? Is that why I chose to forget everything else along with him instead? In my mind, I might have created this fairy tale when he is a beautiful, yet elusive creature, only appearing whenever it suits him.

Typical, except for the mystical creature part. Couldn't I simply imagine him being married? That surely would have done the trick, too. This fantasy definitely didn't help me forget him. Everything else, but not him. Tough luck, I guess.

'Here, at least let me check your temperature.'

Eric's deep voice brings me back to reality (scrap that, *his* reality), and the cool touch of his hand on my forehead forces a tiny moan from my already parted lips. I open my eyes at the notion and for a second his crystal blue pair takes on an emerald hue, just like Sebastian's.

No, this can't be.

But, as soon as the colour appears it vanishes just as quickly. It could have been the light, or my mind playing tricks with me yet again. Yep, I will blame the latter. I pat away Eric's hand, although I must admit, doing so isn't as easy as it ought to be. I'm in love with Sebastian after all, isn't it?

That's what the dreams would suggest, and yet, when I touch Eric, even for a tiny millisecond, his skin electrifies my whole being. I can't explain it, but it's like I can see white light glowing around him, like a beacon. Like a lighthouse calling in its sailors at the end of the day, promising safety and comfort.

One minute I am terrified of this guy, then the next I want to jump into his arms, feeling like I'm betraying the man I'm supposed to be with. Do I feel guilty? Could I have been the one who left, and because I can't get over it and move on, this is my way of seeking redemption? But why the three days? It doesn't add up. None of this does.

'Please. Just let me touch you.'

Eric whispers, sitting down next to me on the floor. My breath hitches, because his eyes are full of sadness, hurt and something else. Yes, desire. I am sure of it. I gulp, nodding slowly and he lets out a shaky breath, reaching for my face. The gentle caress on my right cheek contains more emotion and feeling than any words could at the moment. The way Eric is trying to look after me feels like it's much more than just a stranger looking after a damsel in distress.

You need to hurry, but you can't trust him yet. You don't know everything.

I want to roll my eyes at the voice, but instead I close my eyes. Not a good idea, considering that both Sebastian and the sea-witch swim in front of my mind's vision, scaring me shitless. I still don't have any idea which one of them is in my head, but it could be either or both. Hmm, is the sea-witch my evil mother-in-law?

Yep, right. A fictional merman with fiery hair, one I used to roam the ocean with and have passionate sex on the seabed and his evil mother who is trying to enchant me. Quite poetic and even more idiotic, especially considering that mermaids simply don't exist. But somehow I created this weird and absurd fantasy to cope with the memory loss or the loss of a lover. That must be it. Did I colour my hair this shade to match the fantasy, too? Can a girl be any more pathetic?

Eric suddenly lets out a groan, which in turn shakes me out of my stupor. I look up at him, but instead of the kind man who rescued me, a furious beast is staring back at me. I clear my throat, because I need some noise to put much needed distance between us. Right now I can't tell whether he is going to slap or kiss me, or probably both. What do I know about men anyway? My imaginary boyfriend is a freaking merman.

'Look, Eve. Whoever has done this to you, they will regret it, I swear.'

His voice is calm, but the anger and hurt in his eyes are killing me. He doesn't even know me, and yet he is willing to avenge the bad guys, because he thinks my honour has been compromised. Then he reaches out and tucks a crimson lock behind my ear, lowering his tone to a whisper:

'Just say the words and consider it done. So, who is the guy I have to kill?'

I can't help but shiver, chuckle and moan, all at the same time. The first being a genuine and very much hormonal reaction to his touch, the second to his slightly mocking tone, and the last to the implications behind his words.

'Honestly Eric, I...'

His intense eyes search my face, and his hand rests at the crook of my neck. Shiver, chuckle, moan. Repeat.

'You what, Eve?'

He says my name in such a sensual way and he glances at my parted lips so suggestively that my breath hitches and I close my eyes in anticipation. He pulls me closer gently, resting a hand at the back of my head. It takes an eternity, but his lips brush against mine and my lips begin to tingle. I guess this was easier than I thought.

No, Ariel, you can't let him do it like this. It has to be true love's first kiss for this to work, remember?

I wish I did remember, but the voice snaps me out of it nonetheless. I place a hand on Eric's broad chest, and this time its his turn to repeat my three reactions. In the same order, too. His lips disengage from mine, too, leaving me question this decision as well. Because, right now, all I want is for him to kiss me. What the hell is wrong with me? Can't I make my bloody mind up?

Okay, let's make a list here. Pros and cons. Simple. Sebastian: hot, mysterious, not real. Eric: also sexy, mysterious, could be dangerous, too, and yep, very real. I even reach out to touch his bicep, before his groan lets me know how real he is. I pull away quickly, as if burnt.

I figure that honesty is the best policy here. If he decides I'm crazy, then so be it. I will stay with my fictional boyfriend until his memory fades away, too. I take a deep breath and look deep into Eric's crystal blue eyes. And I want to tell him the truth, I really do. But there is just one problem with that.

As if under a magic spell, as soon as I open my lips to tell Eric the truth (or what I think the truth is), I feel like I'm being sucked out of the room. I imagine this is how being sucked up by a tornado would feel. Everything around me blurs and I'm swirling with the rhythm, round and round till I feel sick. I call out to Eric, but my voice is gone. I simply can't speak and I can't breathe, either. And then, when I think this can't get worse, I'm falling. And that's the last thing I remember before everything disappears.

~o~

Chapter 2

~o~

I take Sebastian's hand, dragging him through the ruins of the old underwater temple. He swims behind me effortlessly, and I can't help but feel giddy inside. This has been my secret hide-out for years, and I'm finally ready to share it with him. I glance back over my shoulder, and the pair of emerald green eyes I know so well glint at me, the rays of the setting sun reflected in them.

I stop, turning around and fully taking in the view. The water always seems like its alive, and although not many know, it is. Myriads of creatures live under the surface, and then another million at the bottom of the ocean, waiting to be discovered. In my bold moments, I talked to Sebastian about all the other oceans we could discover, but he just laughed at me, saying that I was way too ambitious for my own good.

But now, looking at him in the fading light, his eyes heated with desire, I don't think I'm being too ambitious or too childish. I want it all. A pang of sadness clouds this perfect moment, because, right now I realise that showing him my collection will never be enough. Gathering local things that people throw away is just the tip of the iceberg. Just like Sebastian is. But I don't have the heart to tell him that.

Instead I splash him playfully, grabbing his hand again and turning back to my secrets. I feel bad for not being able to share my deepest desires with him anymore, so I do the next best thing: I share my trinkets with him. We swim through the alcoves of the church, and I tell him to duck when I know he would bump his head. Of course, he does so anyway, and then we laugh it off.

It takes us about half an hour of leisurely pace to reach the secret chamber. I stop before the heavy metal doors, glancing back over my shoulders. Part of me wants to swim away and never look back. All the waters of the world are calling out to me, and their call is something that's so hard to resist. But then so is the green pair of eyes that's staring right at me.

My heart is torn between staying and going, and my decision to reveal my secret sanctuary didn't help, either. Sebastian might realise that, too, because his eyes darken a shade and he nods in understanding, pulling me in for a tight hug. A sob escapes me, one created from anger, frustration and sadness. We both know how this will end, and I don't like it.

'You will come back to me. I know you will.'

I cry now, my tears streaming down my face. My mother warned me of this. She, too, left the ocean to find love and adventure, and almost never returned. And when she did, she was different. She no longer wanted the sea, because she was so happy on the shore. I still have no idea whether my father knows or not.

'I won't be the same. We won't be the same.'

I whisper against his muscular chest, inhaling his natural scent. Why do I have to want more? Why isn't this enough? I love him so much it hurts, and yet, I'm being an ungrateful woman, lead by her desire to experience new things. Sebastian sighs against my hair, nuzzling my ear. Desire rushes through my body and I can feel the tingling begin at the base of my tail.

'And that's not an issue. Look. We have been denying you your true nature all these years. I want you to thrive. And trust me, if you do this, our relationship will reach new heights, too.'

He kisses my neck gently, catching me when my tail turns into legs. He doesn't waste any time, placing his other hand between my legs, cupping my clit into his palm. I moan into his chest, holding onto his shoulders.

'You think this is good, hmm?'

He asks, voice smooth and husky, caressing my senses. To accentuate his words, he removes his hand, replacing it with his thumb and forefinger, beginning to rub my clit in tantalizingly slow circles. Because I don't answer him straight away, he inserts a finger into my pussy, curling it upwards. I bite down on his shoulder.

'Now, trust me, if you do what you have to – no, what you w*ant* to – do, we will both enjoy this so much more. Besides...'

He adds, inserting another finger, moving them faster now, in and out of my hole:

'I will be watching you all the time.'

My eyes snap open and I look at him, panting with desire.

'How?'

There is a wicked glint in his eyes and he winks at me the same moment he increases the pace of his fingers, making me cum.

'You have your secrets and so do I. Now get your sexy ass into that vault, so I can fuck it until it's raw.'

I blush at his words, but not anyway, leading the way. Pressing the button is much easier now that I know I have permission to do this. But the real question isn't whether Sebastian will ever forgive me. The real question is whether I can forgive myself.

Because I'm still taking my sweet time (and because it isn't so easy to swim without my tail and fully aroused), Sebastian scoops me up wedding-style, and swims into the vault with me in his arms. His upper arm accidentally brushes one of my nipples and it hardens instantly. I look around at the enormous vault that contains all my trinkets. I can't help but feel the previous excitement return. I clear my throat.

'So, you are going to fuck me in here?'

A blush creeps up my cheeks when he nods, then walks up to the statue that's in the middle of the room. The message is loud and clear and my head begins to spin from the promise and threat of what he is about to do to me. My now human pussy is dripping wet, and my toes tingle in anticipation. I honestly can't wait for him to show me what he is capable of. Because I'm pretty sure I'm about to see a side of Sebastian that I have never seen before. And I'm pretty sure I will like it very much.

~o~

Chapter 3

~o~

When he sets me down at the base of the sculpture, I gulp, facing the handsome human. His features are almost royal, so elegant yet fierce. He is resting one leg on a small pedestal, holding a gun and wearing a sailor's outfit. His deep blue eyes penetrate my soul. My blush deepens when I recall all the times I pleasured myself while looking at this mystery man, and now Sebastian is about to do the same. It feels weird, but somehow, it also feels like fulfilling a hidden fantasy. So many times I wished I could tell him what I truly wanted, what would truly turn me on, but I was too scared. And now, he have guessed and he is willing to do this for me. For both of us.

'Is he the one you want to fuck?'

Sebastian asks, his words making me blush some more. But something else happens, too. We have talked dirty in the past, but never this way. Never about another man. But, as it turns out, bondage and anal sex aren't the only human inventions that are fun and enjoyable. My guilt is mixed with desire, and I nod, tentatively placing my hand on the statue's arm.

'Yes. I would like him to have his way with me.'

Sebastian spanks my ass, pushing me flush up against the statue. Its coldness makes me shiver, and I involuntarily spread my legs for Sebastian as my nipples press onto the hard marble.

'I bet you would. But guess what?'

I glance back over my shoulder, and Sebastian is looking at me with so much hunger that I've never experienced before. It scares me more than my own hunger. Because, if this idea of me having sex with someone else turns us on so much, then what does it say about us?

That you are finally embracing our culture.

My mum's voice suddenly rings in my ears, and I gulp. Sebastian spanks me again, making me bite my lower lip. He then pushes his cock straight into my pussy, without any warning or warming up. I cry out in pain, but he grabs my hair, twisting it around his fist. Slowly, but surely, he turns my head back towards the human statue, so I'm forced to look into his lifeless eyes.

'You will do it on my terms. Is that clear?'

A tear rolls down my cheek in a mixture of shame, lust and confusion, but Sebastian pulls on my hair again, plunging deeper inside my pussy.

'Am I being clear, or have you lost your ability to speak?'

I whimper and he pulls out completely, walking up to one of the shelves along the side of the vault. I hold onto the statue's hand, catching my breath. My pussy is sore, but it isn't like we haven't had such a rough session before. It isn't even the fact that Sebastian is taking the dirty talk to the next level. My heart aches because I know that this is the last time we are doing this, and it should be special. And not this way. We had so many chances to fantasize about a threesome, so why now, when all we should want is each other?

He turns back towards me, holding up one of my trinkets. I whimper again, wanting to tell him that it isn't a sexual toy, but he doesn't seem to care. He snaps the whip against his palm, then motions for me to turn around again. I obey, half aroused still, half scared of what he is going to do if I don't do what he asks.

Sebastian walks up behind me, providing two seaweeds. He busies himself tying my hands to the hands of the statue, one each side, so I'm spread out, facing the mystery man. His voice is as smooth as ever while he works:

'You go out there and find him. And then you make him want to fuck you. You hear me?'

I nod, looking at the statue. Suddenly, it comes to life in front of my mind's eyes, its deep blue eyes glinting at me. Somehow, Sebastian's words manifest and for a moment, it's the mystery guy doing things to me. He is the one tying me up, and then it's his hands that hold the whip inches above the small of my back.

'And then when he is so hard it hurts him, you bring him back here. All you can do is kiss him. But it has to be true love's first kiss. Is that clear?'

I nod again, and the first bite of the whip tingles my skin, just above my ass. Sebastian didn't hit me hard, but it was enough to bring another tear to my eye.

'I want him here when he wants you so bad. So we can fuck you together. Would you like that?'

He asks, while plunging into my pussy once again. I release a desperate sigh, tension building in my core.

'Answer me.'

He whispers, lashing out with the whip again, making me squirm. I cum with such a force it takes me a few moments to come back down, legs shaking. It takes me a while to catch my breath and find my voice, too, but Sebastian is patient this time. He rubs my aching skin, while placing soft kisses onto my back. His movements slow down, too, and now he is making love to me the way I want. Slow. Sensual. Special.

'I'm sorry, my love. I'm so sorry.'

He whispers, caressing my hair. I cum twice more like this, before he releases his own load into my pussy, and then we rest on the floor of the vault, glancing up at the tiny opening in the middle. The rays of the sun have disappeared by now, and a strange feeling settles on my heart. I prop up on one elbow, glancing down at Sebastian's handsome face.

'I know why you did this. Thank you.'

I whisper, another tear rolling down my face. He brushes it away, then grabs my hand and places a soft kiss onto my palm.

'You are welcome, my queen. Now go and fulfil your heart's desire.'

I nod, beaming at him. I now know that what he just did was from pure love. He had to push me to my limits to make me realise what I truly wanted. I know it sounds weird, but I have been denying myself the very thing that would make me whole. And what makes this worse is that I have been denying Sebastian the same.

He deserves to be able to follow the traditions of our people, but because he loves me, he can't. I want to tell him that as the daughter of the sea king, I thought it wouldn't be proper to have more partner than one. But I know that my mother had many lovers, too. And she loved my dad from the bottom of her heart. She loved them all, and together, they formed a family. Sebastian's face suddenly takes on a serious note and he looks away.

'You need to go to the sea-witch early morning.'

I nod, my heart sinking.

'I know. I will miss you so much.'

I say, voice trembling. Sebastian pulls me close, whispering into my ear:

'I will be waiting for you till your return.'

He kisses me deeply and gently, making me forget all the bruises I suffered earlier. In fact, the way he is setting my body on fire makes me want to do some naughty stuff myself. I clear my throat, looking up at the statue. It's almost as if it winks at me in the dim light.

'Do you have more seaweed?'

I ask, a mischievous glint in my eyes. Sebastian laughs, and the sound warms my breaking heart. For a moment I even believe that this could work. I believe that whatever Ursula sets as my price will be worth paying. With a sigh I take the seaweed from Sebastian, tying his hands together, then straddling his hips.

I can feel his erection spring to life once more, but instead of sitting on his shaft, I decide to please him with my tongue and lips instead. I am hell-bent on making our last night as special as it can be. The sea-witch can wait, this can't. Because I have no idea when I will be able to do this again. *If* I will ever be able to do this again...

~o~

Chapter 4

~o~

The tornado sweeps me up again, then spits me out, not just figuratively. Okay, there might not be a tornado per se, but my now constant headaches have turned into daymares. The dreams were bad enough, but this? I am definitely losing my mind. When the picture finally clears, I'm still feeling confused, sad and aroused. Judging by my wet cheeks, the crying wasn't just part of this weird fantasy.

Eric's eyes are on me, and so are his hands. I gulp, trying to push him off me, feeling violated all of a sudden. By Sebastian, by my dreams, by my own desires, and now by Eric. I finally manage to clear my throat.

'Look, I would tell you what happened to me, I really would. The only problem with that is that I don't remember a thing.'

He stays motionless for a moment, but then his eyes grow wide with understanding. Sort of.

'That might be the trauma you went through. Tell me the last thing you recall about what happened and we can figure it out from there.'

I roll my eyes, more at myself than at him. Where do I begin? Shall I tell him about the kinky sex I've been having with a merman, while getting permission from him – no, an order, actually – to come and fuck Eric? I didn't think so. I shake my head.

'That's just it, I can't. Purely because I don't remember anything. As in nada. Not even my name or where I come from or...'

I trail off, feeling embarrassed all of a sudden. Do I tell him about the dreams? Maybe if he knew what was going on, he could help...

Don't you dare.

Okay, so that settles that. Eric gets up from his spot by my side on the sofa and starts pacing the room. I get a whiff of his scent, and the room begins to spin once again. Although for a different reason this time (thank the Gods). Of course, being a good girl, I give him time to process. And that's when I notice the elderly man who's sitting at a dining table at the far end, sipping what looks like tea.

Not creepy at all.

As if sensing being the centre of my attention (yep, totally normal), he glances towards me, and his frown slowly turns into a broad smile as he raises his cup at me. I nod absent-mindedly. Where have I seen him before? He is unusual in a way, and yet so familiar, just like everything else about this whole thing. He is wearing a navy jacket, paired with black pants and what I would describe as mannequin shoes. They are pointy, shiny and by the looks of them, very expensive. The kind movie stars would wear, you know. Yeah, I guess you know better than I do anyway.

'Eve, is it?'

The strange man asks before taking a sip from his tea. The room is so quiet that you could hear a pin drop. It's almost eerie, really. Not to mention that the question now hangs between us. Is it Eve? Or Ariel? And just how much can I trust these men to reveal what I now believe to be the truth? No, I might have lost my memories, but something about this just doesn't feel right. It just doesn't...

Eric's voice forces its way into my subconscious, way before the meaning of his words reach my brain.

'Dad, would you excuse us for a minute, please?'

Dad... Okay, kind of makes sense and reduces the weirdness of this situation. Shame washes over me as I realize that my unwelcome interlude must have interrupted the family breakfast. Eric Senior nods, then leaves without a word. I glance at Eric, who is standing by the bay window. I can faintly hear the sound of seagulls, crying out in the increasing wind. Interesting enough, I think I can hear my own ragged breathing, too. Not to mention the loud thumping of my heart. Mentioned organ threatens to jump through my throat and out of my body at the deafening sound of the key turning in the lock. Okay, part of me is finding this sexy and arousing, but I'm not naïve. At least I don't think I am.

'Are you sure you don't remember? You don't remember how...'

His voice is husky; painful even. For a brief moment Sebastian's image pops to mind, and as Eric's voice trails off, I sort of have a vision. His hair miraculously changes colour, and instead of the (very) tight dress pants he is wearing now, all there is is a fluorescent emerald tail...

'Eve...'

I blink, only to realize that Eric is towering over me now. There is no trace of the transformation he went through a moment ago, but there is way more evidence of his sudden arousal, which takes me by surprise. His hooded blue gaze travels down the length of my body and I feel naked yet again. Except, I don't mind this time.

What the hell do you think you are doing?

I push the voice away, completely lost in the azure pair of eyes staring at me. Then, as I look deeper, they turn to green. Nope. Na-ah. I snap out of my stupor, placing both hands onto Eric's chest, trying to push him off me. He doesn't budge, and panic takes over my body. I freeze as he sweeps a stray strand of hair off my shoulder. His eyes seem distant, as if he was lost in a memory. Is this how I looked when I was daydreaming?

'Do you know how long I have been waiting for you?'

I blink at his admission, baffled by its meaning. I raise an eyebrow at him, prompting him to continue. The alarm bells are loud and clear, but I silence them for now. He nods, absent-mindedly caressing my hair.

'I knew you would come eventually. I just had to wait for the right time. And, here you are. Too bad you don't remember *anything*.'

Oh my god. Does he have something to do with my memory loss? I clear my throat, my eyes searching for an escape route. Just in case he is a serial killer, you know.

'Wh-what do you mean you knew I would come? Do we know each other?'

He lets out a frustrated sigh, then leans in, placing a kiss onto my forehead.

'Not as much as I would like.'

He moves down lower, placing another lingering kiss behind my ear, and an involuntary moan escapes me. No, I can't let him do this. Not like this. He isn't in love with me. He can't be. And I'm not in love with him, either. I decide to push my luck.

'How do we know each other then?'

He rests his forehead against mine for a second, closing his eyes.

'You honestly don't remember?'

I shake my head. Well, as much as I can with his weight on top of me.

'Fine. I will tell you how we met for the first time then.'

I furrow my brows, but probably sensing my confusion, he adds, getting up and slowly walking back towards the window.

'No, not after whatever accident happened to you. We met long before that.'

He pauses, looking out at the sea. A seagull screams in the background. Another one answers. Why does it sound like a warning? Eric clears his throat, then turns towards me. My eyes go wide when I notice the tears that started streaming down his face.

'You saved my life, and I've been trying to find you ever since.'

He turns back to the window, but before I could process what he just said, he adds:

'And now that I have, I don't intend to let you slip away again.'

I want to ask him if that's a threat, but I don't get the chance. The headache starts at the back of my skull, then in the matter of seconds I black out. The last thing that plays on my mind is what I thought I heard the seagull scream:

Run!

Crazy, right?

~o~

A tempting taste of other, bite-size erotica, from the naughty pen of Timea Tokes:

~o~

A SPECIAL CUP OF COFFEE
(SAMPLE)

Don't worry, this is a first for me, too..."
Ah, is that supposed to comfort me?
Very promising.

I try to pull on the restraints, but he has tied me up tightly. My heart is pounding, and I can't see a thing because of the blindfold. All I can do is wait helplessly until he figures out his next move, wondering how could I have gotten myself into this mess.

A mere hour ago I was sitting at the bar, minding my own business, drinking heavily, as if there was no tomorrow. Right up to the moment when the bartender offered to make me a special cup of coffee. Which I'm still waiting for, by the way.

Just saying.

Okay, I wasn't that naïve to think that we would actually be drinking coffee, cuddling on his couch, no. And as I said, I didn't want that anyway. I wanted hot, steamy, and kinky sex. And although he hasn't touched me yet, not in that way anyway, this whole situation is kinky alright.

"Just try to relax and clear your mind..."

He is really getting into this. Does he have a guidebook that he is citing from? I must admit that hearing his voice alone makes me shiver all over. It is sexy as hell, and I can already feel the previous dampness of my thong worsening by the minute. I wonder how long is he going to keep me suspended like this? It's funny how you lose all of your senses when you can't see.

No kidding!

Although I can hear his voice, but only when he allows me to, and I still can't tell where it's coming from. For all I know he could be standing in the doorway, ready to lock me in, leaving me to suffer for God knows how long. I sure as hell hope he isn't planning to make that special cup of coffee *right now.*

But judging by what he just said, I guess I need to do the opposite. In fact, my mind is the only thing that's working perfectly well right now. And my survival instincts, of course. I begin to regret that I didn't listen to my friends. I should have waited for this kind of kink until I knew the guy, let alone trusted him.

Oh my God, I don't even know his name!

"You might feel a little bit cold. Try not to wiggle too much, okay?"

Okay, I was wrong. All my nerves are on edge, and I want to scream from the ice-cold sensation that's burning my left nipple right now.

Little bit cold?

Whatever he put on me makes me want to swear and scream, except I can't. All I can give out is a tiny whimper through my gritted teeth. I want to tell him to stop, to let me go, feeling embarrassed and exposed all of a sudden.

But as quickly as the thought forms in the back of my mind, it evaporates just as quickly when he takes my erect nipple into his mouth. His hot, wet tongue is a relief from the ice-cold sensation, and yet it feels a tad bit more painful, maybe because I am more sensitive than I ever was. He bites down gently, and I can feel the coldness on my right nipple, while he is stroking my left one with his tongue.

I gasp, getting lost in the mixed sensations of hot and cold, pain and pleasure. But it doesn't last long, and as much as I wanted him to stop at first, now I wish that he would continue the sweet torture. An involuntary moan leaves my lips, and he lets out a small chuckle.

"Don't worry, I have only just started."

His words send a jolt of electricity right down to my lady parts, and I'm sure I blush a little, too. I think about my black strapless dress, the black lace push-up bra and the black high heels scattered around the room. I'm not even sure he is wearing anything right now, as after a few passionate kisses, he moved straight onto the subject. He promised it to be fun, erotic and orgasmic.

The last part convinced me, and I'm more and more sure that he is a man who keeps his promises...

~o~

Kiss & Tell Tail
Reverse Harem Fairy Tales
1
Timea Tokes

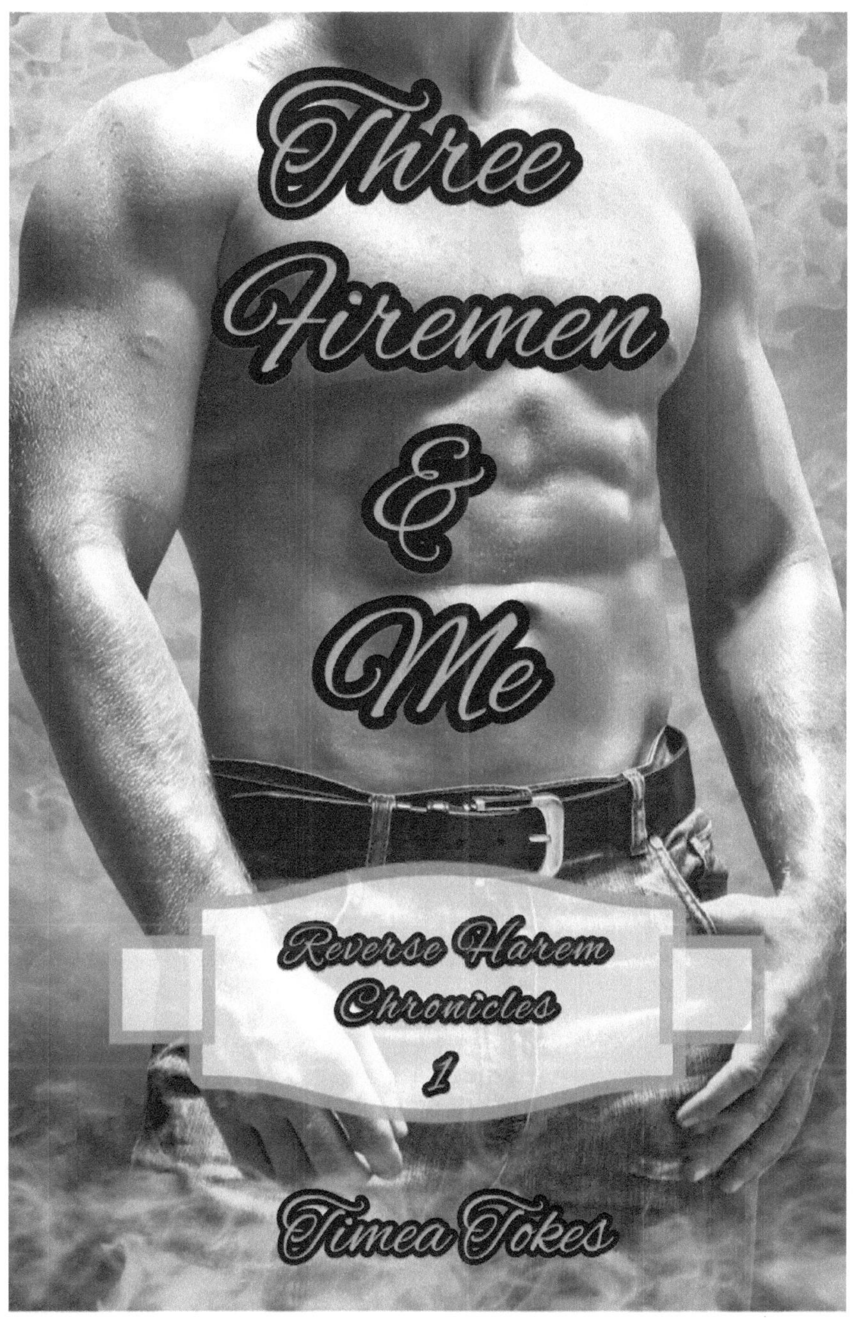

Three
Firemen
&
Me
Reverse Harem
Chronicles
1
Timea Tokes

How About the Rooftop?
Don't Make A Sound

Paranormal Erotica:
Conjured Lover

The Plumber Series:
Seducing the Plumber 1: Sweet Time Waiting
Seducing the Plumber 2: Sweet Torture

The Escort Series:
The Escort's Taxi Ride
The Escort's Taxi Ride 2
The Escort's Taxi Ride 3

The Good Neighbor Series (Bisexual, Why Choose):
The Good Neighbor – An Unexpected Threesome
The Good Neighbor – Tied up by the Knight
The Good Neighbor – In the Backseat
The Good Neighbor – The Massage
The Good Neighbor – Guilty Pleasures

Sweet yet Naughty:
Forgotten
Blue Highlights

Gay:
The Stranger

Collections of Short Stories:
You Had Me At Kinky
You Had Me At Steamy
You Had Me At Rough

Coming Soon:

The Plumber's Excuse (2020)
Three Billionaires & Me (2020)
Kiss & Tell Tail 3 (2020)
A Cupid Mistake (2021)
Hell's Bride (2021)

Follow Timea Tokes on:

Amazon @timea_tokes

Twitter @timea_tokes

Facebook @herfirstsecret

Goodreads @timea_tokes

Sign up to her newsletter, and have a look at her blog for more bite-size erotica, paranormal romance, reviews and more:

www.timeatokes.com

<u>Note from the Author, Timea Tokes:</u>

~o~

My dear, lovely Reader, thank you for taking the time to read my story! I really hope you enjoyed it as much as I did writing it. As always, your feedback is highly valued and much appreciated.

Please do take the time to scroll to the end of the book and leave a review. It would mean the World to me!

And remember, this story is all about your pleasure.

On the next page, you can learn a bit more about me and why I write, but you will also find author interviews (and much more) on my website.

~o~

ABOUT THE AUTHOR

~o~

I have been writing short stories and poems since a young age, but my ultimate goal was creating a novel. Or a series, rather. Now, with my four paranormal romance novels published, as well as more than 30 erotica titles under my belt, , I think I can say that it came true - but this only fuels my desire to write more. After all, we are allowed to dream the same dream (over and over again) - and that's exactly what I'm planning to do :)

I enjoy helping people in any way possible, and I really hope that my books will prove to be inspirational in a way. Whether readers are looking for a swift (and steamy) erotic story, or a paranormal romance, I want them to associate themselves with my characters and realize stuff about themselves in the process.

Yes, even the bad things. Because, in life, there is no black and white, only colors. Therefore, I don't think any of my characters are either good or bad, but rather a little bit of both.

Aren't we all?

Well, if you never had guilty thoughts, never had any self-confidence issues, or if you never wanted something (or someone) who belonged to someone else, then probably my books won't be for you. But, who knows, I might be able to show you a different perspective. I like to experiment with different genres, and new concepts and ideas.

I really enjoy learning as much as I can about people, what makes them tick (and live, laugh, cry, and sigh). In fact, I think our World (and those beyond) are so diverse, ten thousand lifetimes wouldn't be enough to explore it all. But one thing I truly believe in: those who belong in your life will find a way there. Therefore my stories are usually based on chance encounters and ordinary events that take an unexpected turn.

Like a blind date on Valentine's day, or a haircut, or a new job. Who says you can't meet someone 'accidentally'; while going to the hairdresser, someone you lost contact with 500 years ago? Trust me, you can. You just need to brace every day (and every book) with open eyes - and an open heart.

Just remember: my stories are all about you, and you alone. If they capture your attention (and your heart), then I've done my 'job'. I regularly try to release new content, both on Amazon and my blog. Please feel free to have a look, and sign up to my newsletter.

And, just so you know: I care about your opinion, very much so. Whether you liked my work or you didn't, I would be honored if you let me know what it meant for you. It would mean the world to me!

~o~

1. *When did you create your first erotica story, and what was it about?*

Well, my first story wasn't fully erotica, more a romance story. In fact, I never thought that one day I would write anything steamy. Not at all. I was shy, and grew up in an environment, where everything was taboo. Sharing my views on sex with anyone, let alone write about it? No way...

And yet, I soon had to realize that writing romantic stories couldn't happen without the couple getting it on eventually. Especially because the first four books series I created was about the same characters, and they are 100 pages each (which is a lot to go without including a sex scene every now and again). I must admit, I delayed the inevitable for as long as I could, just to realize later how much I enjoyed writing about sex.

Although my first attempts were very timid indeed, I tried to avoid being too explicit or descriptive. I concentrated on the romantic and paranormal aspect of it (the main characters dream about each other, and somehow when I was writing about the dreams, they gave me courage to be a bit braver).

But it wasn't until I started writing my erotic short stories in 2015, when I started to experiment. Well, if you have a look at 'The Good Neighbour', you can see how my explicitness and mood changed throughout the series.

I think I can say that this was the very first fully erotic story I created, fulfilling one of my secret fantasies (no, I don't have a hot neighbour, or at least I don't think I have, but the idea always fascinated me).

2. What (or who) inspired you to start writing erotica?

My own lack of courage, if I'm honest. All my friends were so open about their relationships and their fantasies, so I thought:

"Why do I have to be this way, when I want to explore everything that's out there?"

And as I have always enjoyed writing, I decided to try it out on paper. It started as a therapy I prescribed for myself, and then it escalated, taking me to places I never thought I would visit. I must say that I'm really glad I gave in to temptation.

3. What do you find most challenging when writing these stories?

To let them go when I finish writing them. I believe that it isn't possible, especially when I create a longer story. The characters, the feelings stay with me long after, as they become part of me for at least a little while.

Another aspect of it is that I keep thinking about what others read into them, and whether they convey their meaning in a way that I intended them to. But, just like when you give birth to a child, when writing a story as well you need to give it space after some time.

I once read a quotation (not sure where, or who said it, but it made me smile and I could definitely relate):

"I met the man of my dreams last night.. in chapter five…" *Sigh*

4. Do you write in other genres, and if yes, then would you consider mixing them with erotica?

Yes, and not sure. I ghost-write for a living, as well as create my own stories, which include romance, horror, thriller, fantasy, crime and more, but I'm not sure it would feel right to mix them with erotica. Mind that, I have had some strange requests that were a mixture, like fetish-horror, but it didn't actually include erotica. I suppose it could have, as it was about a foot fetish, which seems to be quite popular. Oh well, another thing to look at in the future :)

My favourite ones are psychological thrillers though, so I could probably turn one of those into erotica, but at the moment I'm thinking of a transition, rather than a mix. So, for example it would start as a thriller, but have a sexual ending. Hmm…

5. Have you written any stories that were inspired by real life events?

Yes. In fact, my very first story, 'Her First and Last Secret Admirer' (the four books I mentioned earlier) started with an actual recurring medieval dream, which I then implemented into the plot, creating a story and background for it. If it wasn't for that urge to put the whole thing into writing, I probably would never have picked up the courage to write at all. Now it is both in print and on Kindle, so I guess it was a nice bargain :)

I think that writing about real events, twisting them a little, but still keeping them close to your heart is an important process.

Also, that way you can relive those events over and over again, and others will keep guessing what was the real part in it.

Strangely enough, it adds to its mystery (and excitement, of course)...

6. What is your speciality and why?

I would say it's mixing the past with the present. I'm not an expert, but I also love to keep up the suspense until the end. Although this doesn't always come through in my erotic stories, as they are linear, but in my paranormal romance books, I draw a parallel between what happened 500 years ago and what's happening right now. It's difficult to explain without revealing the plot itself, but I do love to play with the mind of the reader, if you know what I mean.

7. Are there any topics you don't like writing about?

Now? Not really. If you asked me a few years ago, I would have said everything that involves sex ;)

I guess I just realized that I shouldn't say no, just because I don't know how something feels. If I don't try it, I will never know... If I'm not familiar with a topic, then

I do my research, but not too many things scare me nowadays (without wanting to sound weird or vain).

32

8. Do you have any tips / warnings for newbie erotica writers?

Follow your dreams. You will get some ugly feedback (or none at all), but that doesn't mean that your work isn't appreciated. Don't take them personally, but accept them, so that they can serve as stepping stones, helping you improve your writing. We all make mistakes; that's what makes us human.

Personally, I couldn't wait to grab a physical copy of my books, and that made up for whatever negativity I got (but luckily it has only been minor stuff so far).

So, if you are thinking about writing, or if you already have a story or two, try to make them into a book, no matter how tiny it is. Trust me, as soon as you have it on your shelf, you will become a different person.

9. What is your favourite season and why?

Spring, because that's when everything comes to life. I just love to watch the flowers blossom and the world wake up from its winter slumber. I always feel like I'm reborn myself every time springs comes (I know, I'm a hopeless romantic).